P9-CQS-800

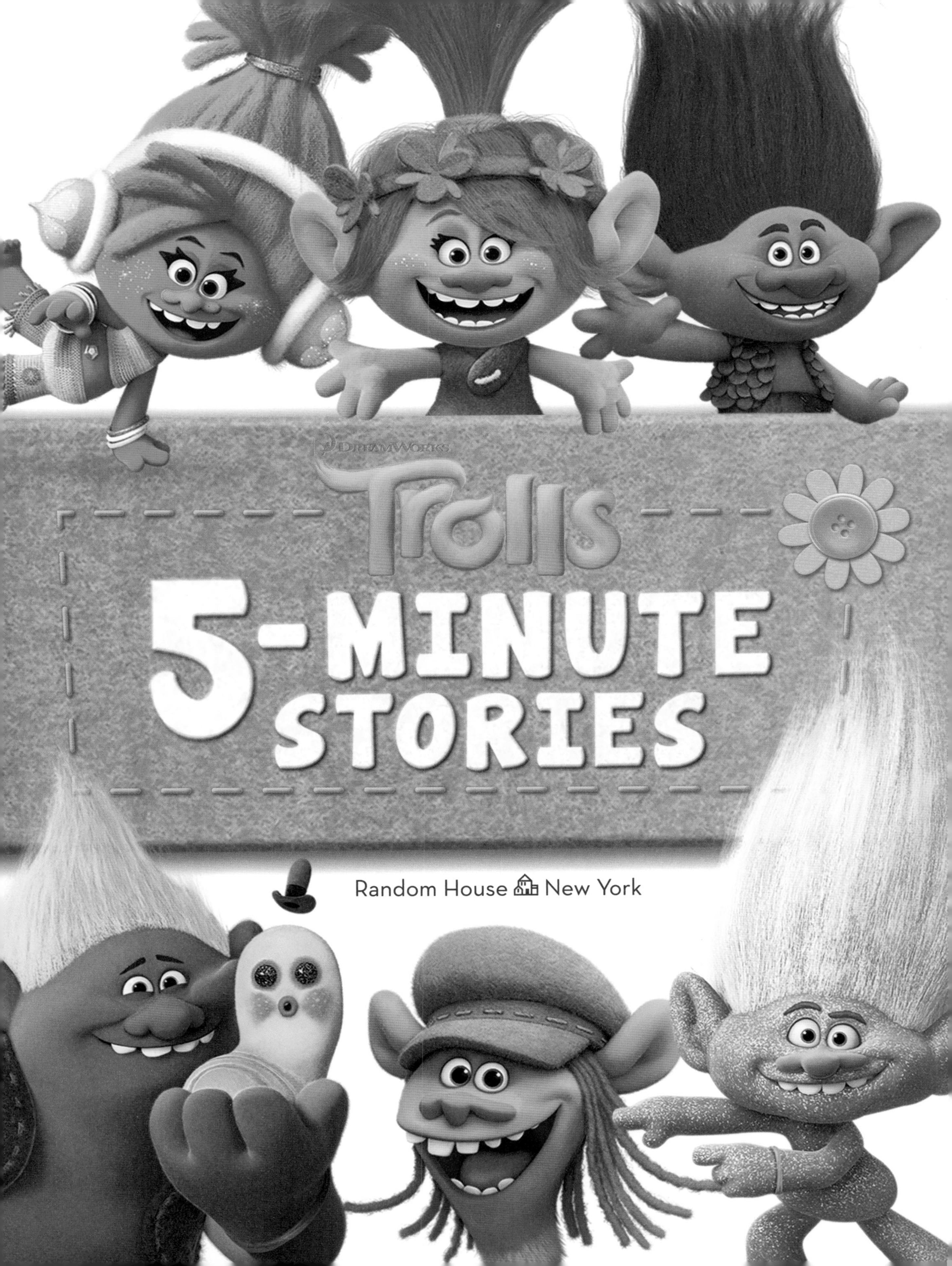
DreamWorks
Trolls
5-MINUTE STORIES
Random House New York

 Published in the United States by Random House Children's Books, a division of Penguin Random House LLC, 1745 Broadway, New York, NY 10019, and in Canada by Penguin Random House Canada Limited, Toronto. The stories contained in this work were originally published separately in slightly different form by Golden Books as *Trolls* in 2016, and by Random House Books for Young Readers as *Dance! Hug! Sing!* in 2016; *Drop the Beat!* in 2017; *Pet Problem!* in 2017; *Everything That Glitters Is Guy!* in 2017; *Out of Branch's Bunker* in 2016; *The Sound of Spring* in 2018; and *Happy Troll-o-ween!* in 2017.
Random House and the colophon are registered trademarks of Penguin Random House LLC.
rhcbooks.com
ISBN 978-1-5247-7266-6 (trade) — ISBN 978-1-5247-7267-3 (ebook)
MANUFACTURED IN CHINA
10 9 8 7 6 5 4 3 2 1

CONTENTS

TROLLS 1

DANCE! HUG! SING! 25

DROP THE BEAT! 41

PET PROBLEM! 59

EVERYTHING THAT GLITTERS IS GUY! 75

OUT OF BRANCH'S BUNKER 91

THE SOUND OF SPRING 115

HAPPY TROLL-O-WEEN! 133

Adapted by Mary Man-Kong
Illustrated by Priscilla Wong

Once upon a time, in a happy forest filled with happy trees, there lived the happiest creatures the world had ever known: the Trolls. They loved nothing more than to

sing

and **dance**

and **hug**

and sing
and dance
and hug—
a lot.

Today was an especially happy day in Troll Village. Princess Poppy was going to throw a big party!

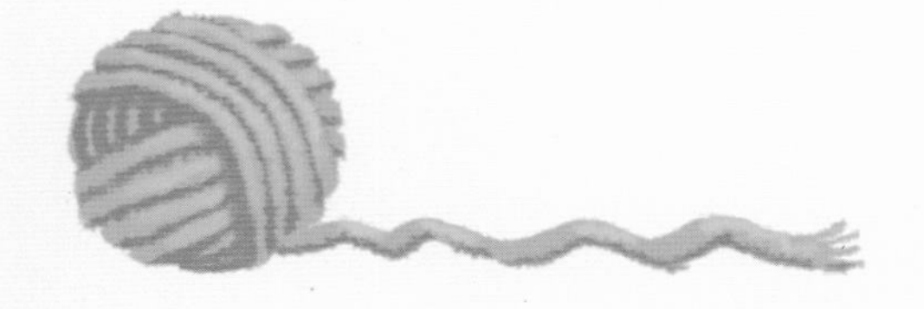

Everyone was excited to celebrate—except Branch. He didn't like singing, dancing, or hugging. Instead, he spent his time worrying about the Bergens.

Long ago, the Bergens had captured Trolls and **eaten** them! The Bergens thought that eating Trolls brought them happiness. Luckily, many of the Trolls had escaped . . .

. . . until now.

Princess Poppy's celebration was the biggest, loudest, craziest party ever! It was so loud that the Bergen Chef found where the Trolls had been living all these years.

Most of the
Trolls
managed to hide.

But Chef was able to scoop up several of them, including Poppy's closest friends, Satin and Chenille, Cooper, Biggie, Guy Diamond, Smidge, DJ Suki, and Creek.

Chef couldn't wait to bring the tasty Trolls back to Bergen Town.

Poppy had to save her friends! She convinced Branch to help her.

Of course, Poppy's plan included making a scrapbook page—with plenty of glitter!

Meanwhile, thanks to Chef, King Gristle would finally get to eat a Troll—and experience happiness! The king decided to have a big celebration called Trollstice so all the Bergens could eat Trolls and become happy, too.

When Poppy and Branch got to King Gristle's castle, they found most of their friends hidden in a cage in Bridget the maid's room.

But Creek was missing. Bridget agreed to help them find Creek if they could get King Gristle to notice her.

Poppy knew what to do. Satin and Chenille made Bridget a glitter jumpsuit. Then all the Trolls sat on her head to make a

SUPER-COLORFUL RAINBOW WIG.

Bridget loved her makeover. She called herself Lady Glittersparkles. The king would certainly notice her now!

When King Gristle saw Lady Glittersparkles, he fell in love. He didn't realize she was his maid. The king took her roller-skating.

He showed her his new locket.

Creek was inside it!

Later, the Trolls snuck into the king's room to save Creek. They grabbed the locket and

But when Poppy opened the locket, Creek wasn't there! Poppy was sad to learn that to save his own life, Creek had told Chef where all the other Trolls of Troll Village were hiding.

How could Creek have betrayed his friends?

Then everyone was trapped in a pot! Poppy lost all hope, and her color started to **fade**.

The other Trolls lost their color, too—they turned gray with sadness.

Suddenly, they heard a beautiful voice singing. It was Branch! His singing brought out his true colors—he turned bright green with purple hair.

He sang because his heart was full of the hope and joy that Poppy had showed him. He loved Poppy, and Poppy loved Branch. She and the other Trolls started to sing, too, and their true colors came back.

Bridget couldn't let the Bergens eat her friends. She lifted the cover off the pot so the Trolls could escape. Bridget knew she would get in trouble, but she was glad she'd had one day of happiness on her date with the king.

At Trollstice, the Bergens, eager to finally get a taste of happiness, were angry to discover that Bridget had set the Trolls free.

Just then, the Trolls burst in to save her. They formed the **rainbow wig** again . . .

. . . and landed right on Bridget's head.

When King Gristle learned that Lady Glittersparkles was actually Bridget, he was overjoyed. He realized that he didn't need to eat a Troll to be happy.

All he needed was a full heart and Bridget by his side. "They do look kind of happy," one Bergen admitted.

Branch told everyone how miserable he'd been until Poppy had taught him how to dance and hug and sing. Before long, all the Bergens were dancing and singing, too.

The only Bergen who wasn't happy was Chef. Now that no one wanted to eat Trolls, she was out of a job! Chef and Creek were banished from Bergen Town, destined to be unhappy together.

The Trolls had brought happiness to Bergen Town, but not in a way anyone had expected. The Trolls had a huge celebration. Poppy was crowned queen of the Trolls, and everyone cheered.

After finally experiencing their true colors, the Bergens and the Trolls now lived in **peaceful** harmony.

By Rachel Chlebowski

Hi!
Welcome to Troll Village! I'm
Poppy, and my favorite things are
singing, dancing, scrapbooking, and HUGGING!
Here in Troll Village, we celebrate
Hug Time every hour on the hour, and
we sing and dance and hug and
dance and sing ALL the TIME!
Why say it when you can sing it?

By now you are probably asking yourself, "Who or what is a Troll?" We're only the happiest, most *hair*-tastic group of best friends in the whole universe!
Poppy, why don't you introduce your friends?

Biggie is my biggest best friend in Troll Village. He's also the biggest softie. He loves to dress up his pet, Mr. Dinkles, for photo shoots. How cute!
Fun Facts About Biggie
• He cries happy tears.
• He's a fan of the short-vest look.
• His fave snack: Mr. Dinkles' cupcakes!

Cooper has the **CRAZIEST** dance moves and always exudes *pop*-timistic enthusiasm! Cooper is upbeat and friendly and plays a mean harmonica solo—meaning he's wicked good, and actually the complete opposite of mean! And he's not wicked. He's good. Oh . . . you know what I mean!
Fun Facts About Cooper
• He has four legs for happy dancing.
• He's covered with Troll hair!
Shhh . . . Keep it down. Do you want the Bergens to hear you?

Smidge is super small and cute, but don't let that fool you. She has the strongest hair and the biggest voice!

Fun Facts About Smidge

- **Working out is her way of life.**
- **She can jump rope with her own hair!**
- **Her hobbies include listening to heavy-metal music and crocheting.**

This guy makes Troll Village sparkle! **Guy Diamond** is 100 percent *glitter*-rific 100 percent of the time—and 100 percent naked 100 percent of the time! Guy Diamond loves parties and leaves glitter wherever he goes.

Fun Facts About Guy Diamond

- **He shakes off a cloud of glitter when he dances.**
- **He's pretty much a living disco ball!**

You're awesome!
No, you are!

Satin and **Chenille** are BFFFs—Best Fashion Friends Forever! These Trolls are twins, but they never wear the same outfit at the same time.

Fun Facts About Satin and Chenille

- **Satin is pink, and Chenille is blue.**
- **They know everything fashion.**
- **They're connected at the hair!**

I want to wear EVERYTHING they make!

My friend DJ Suki is Troll Village's resident mash-up expert. Trolls can't help shaking their hair when DJ Suki is around!
Fun Facts About DJ Suki
• She owns all-natural DJ equipment.
• She mixes and scratches with her funky Wooferbug!

Creek is a gem—
because he's precious to everyone
in Troll Village! He always knows what
to say and sing. He's also a groovy
dance partner and a great
yoga teacher!
Fun Facts
About Creek
• He's calm and collected.
• His freckles are made
of glitter!

Fuzzbert
is an adorable Troll wrapped entirely in hair. His hair shakes when he laughs, and he can use his entire body for tickling his friends!
Fun Facts About Fuzzbert
• He speaks his own language.
• He's all hair, all the time!
Fuzzbert loves to dance. His nickname is Twinkle Toes!

Harper

uses her hair like a giant paintbrush, so she's always covered in paint from head to toe. No canvas is too small for Harper when it comes to letting her true colors shine!

Fun Facts About Harper

- **She would rather create than chat.**
- **She uses her art to express herself.**
- **Her smock is always spotless!**

isn't like the other Trolls. He's very cautious. He's worried that the hungry Bergens will find us, so he's always prepared.

Fun Facts About Branch

- **He's practical.**
- **He has a highly camouflaged, heavily fortified Bergen-proof survival bunker.**

Why are you telling them all this? It could get out to the Bergens!

We Trolls come in all shapes and sizes, but one thing is for sure: we all have a lot of heart . . . and a lot of hair!
Welcome to Troll Village
• Heart: Maximum capacity!
• Hair: Record-breaking highs!

DRØP the BEAT!

By David Lewman
Illustrated by Gabriella Matta and Fabio Laguna

It was a beautiful day in Troll Village. The sun was shining, the birds were singing, and there was music in the air—coming from DJ Suki! She was playing some new music on her Wooferbug. The Wooferbug thumped and pumped to the beat.

Biggie loved the music. He started shaking his hair, and Mr. Dinkles bobbed his head.

"Hey," Biggie called to DJ Suki. "What are you doing?"

"I'm dropping the beat to a new song," DJ Suki said. Dropping the beat meant she had started the music.

Biggie and Mr. Dinkles were confused. They thought dropping the beat meant that DJ Suki had lost it!

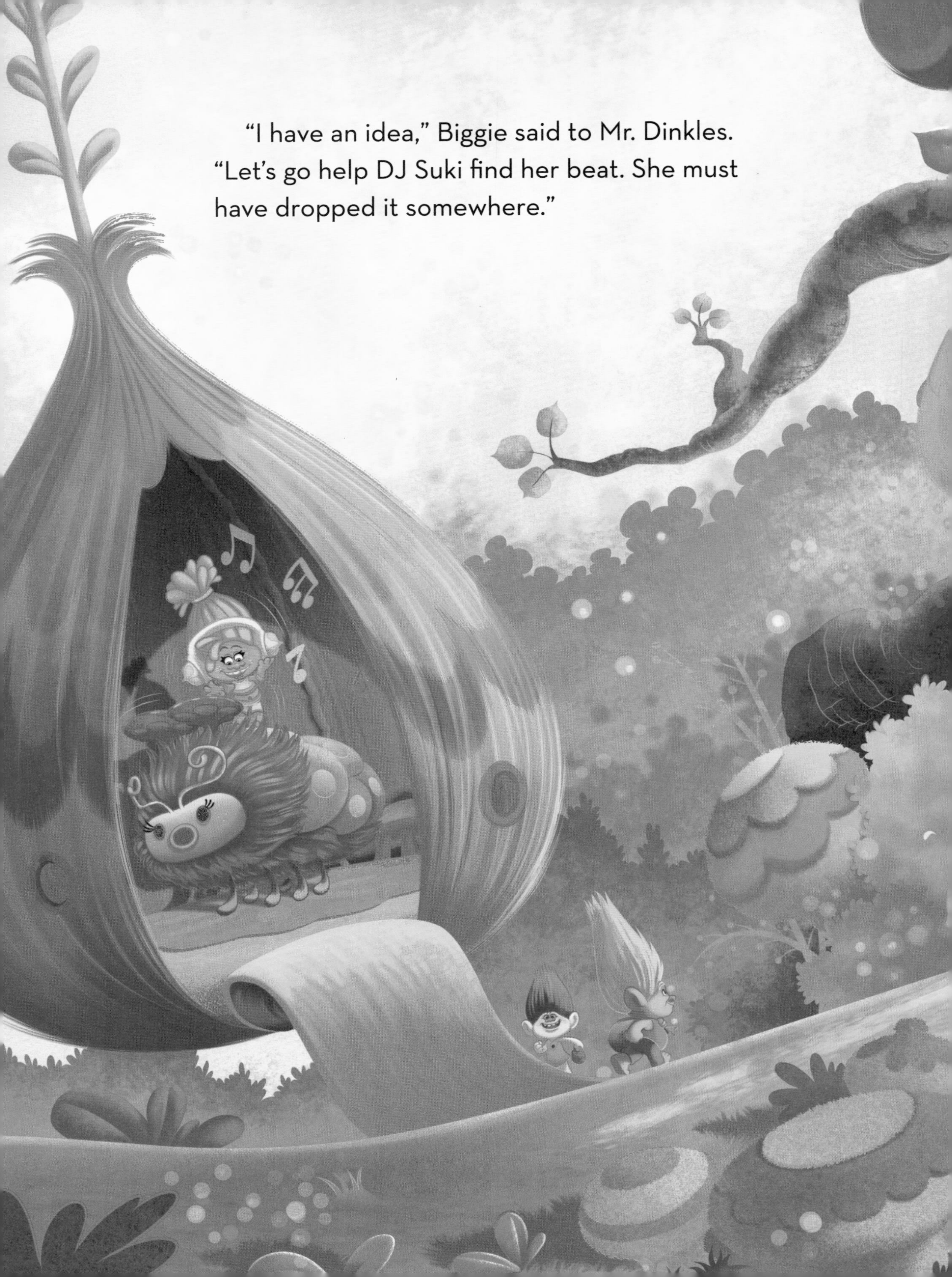

"I have an idea," Biggie said to Mr. Dinkles. "Let's go help DJ Suki find her beat. She must have dropped it somewhere."

They decided to start looking in Troll Village. On the way, they bumped into their friend Cooper.

"DJ Suki dropped her beat," Biggie said to Cooper. "And we're going to help her look for it. Have you seen it anywhere?"

Cooper shook his head. "But if she needs some music, I can play my harmonica," he said. He started playing it, and danced happily.

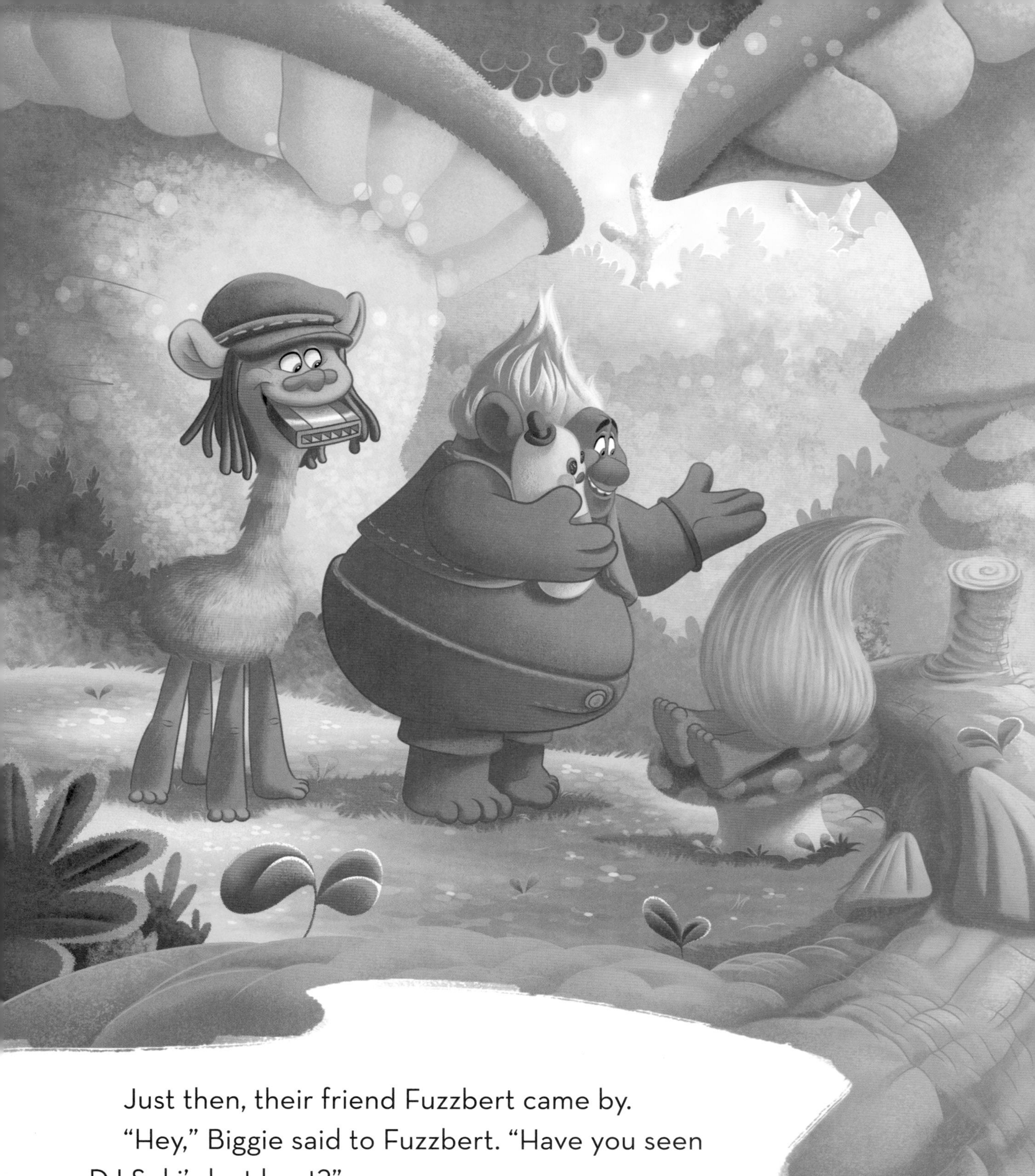

Just then, their friend Fuzzbert came by.

"Hey," Biggie said to Fuzzbert. "Have you seen DJ Suki's lost beat?"

Fuzzbert shook his head. He started to hum and whistle along with Cooper's harmonica, and Biggie clapped his hands.

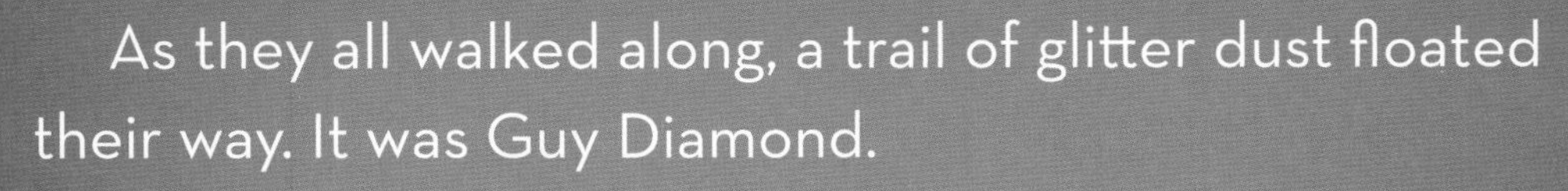

As they all walked along, a trail of glitter dust floated their way. It was Guy Diamond.

"Hey," Biggie said to him. "We're looking for DJ Suki's beat. Have you seen it?"

"No," said Guy Diamond, listening to their music. "But I do love to sing." He cleared his throat. *"La, la, la, la, la, la, la . . ."*

"Sounds great!" Biggie said. "Why don't you come along with us?"

Biggie and his friends continued on, then stopped at Satin and Chenille's pod. They were busy making a new outfit for a party.

"Hey," Biggie said. "Have you seen DJ Suki's lost beat?"

Satin and Chenille hadn't seen it, but they were willing to help.

They heard Cooper playing his harmonica, Fuzzbert humming, Biggie clapping, and Guy Diamond singing, so they decided to sing harmony.

Next, Biggie and his friends stopped by Poppy's pod. She was busy with her scrapbooking.

"What's going on?" she asked.

"We're looking for DJ Suki's beat," said Biggie. "Have you seen it?

"Sorry, but I haven't," said Poppy. Then she heard her friends' song.

"Wow! That sounds *Troll*-rific!" she said. "I can add to your song by playing my cowbell."

Clang! Clang! Clang!

It sounded like music to everyone's ears!

The Trolls headed back to DJ Suki's studio.

"Sorry you dropped your beat," Biggie said to DJ Suki. "We all tried to look for it, but we couldn't find it. We did find a whole bunch of wonderful sounds along the way!"

DJ Suki loved her friends' new music.

"Dropping the beat doesn't mean losing it," she said. "Dropping the beat just means I'm starting to play a new song."

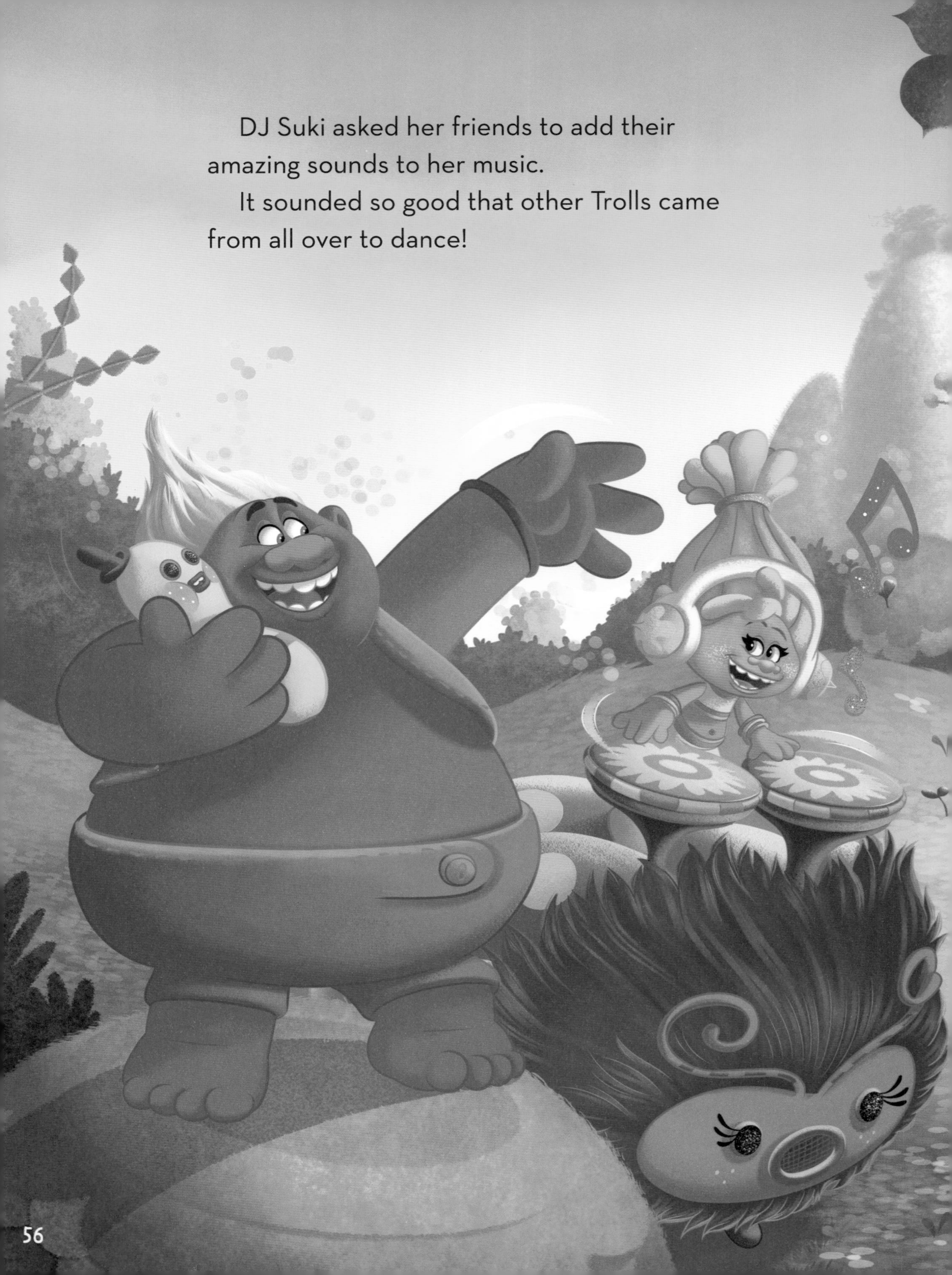

DJ Suki asked her friends to add their amazing sounds to her music.

It sounded so good that other Trolls came from all over to dance!

They played, danced,
and sang all night long
to the best beat ever!

By David Lewman

Illustrated by Fabio Laguna and Grace Mills

Ginger Jo loved animals. ALL animals! So naturally, she loved working at the Troll Village pet nursery. All day long, she got to take care of baby critters, from Wooferbugs to Sparkleflies to Humworms.

Poppy often visited the nursery to help her friend. One day, she stuck her head in the door and asked, "Hey, Ginger Jo! Got room for one more?"

"Sure, Poppy!" Ginger Jo said. "What is it? A Tunebug? A Glowfly? A Fuzzy Wuzzbert?"

"No," Poppy replied, "it's a . . ."

". . . Tarantapuff!" Sure enough, Poppy brought in a fuzzy baby Tarantapuff. "Will you help me take care of it? I call him Sweetpuff 'cause he's so sweet!"

Ginger Jo was surprised. Full-grown Tarantapuffs were big, hairy spider-like critters that usually lived deep in the dark forest. She'd never heard of anyone keeping a Tarantapuff as a pet. But she really did love ALL animals. . . .

"Of course I'll help you!" Ginger Jo said. "Does Sweetpuff like it when you pet him?"

"He loves it!" Poppy said. "Give it a try!"

Secretly, Ginger Jo was a little afraid to pet the Tarantapuff. But when she stroked his hair, he leaned against her and purred!

"Oh, Sweetpuff really is sweet!" she exclaimed. "And so soft!"

But Ginger Jo and Poppy quickly found out it wasn't easy taking care of a big baby Tarantapuff.

Sweetpuff was very hungry—all the time!

Even though Ginger Jo and Poppy gave him lots of food, it was hard to keep theTarantapuff from gobbling up all the other animals' food, too.

"This is one hungry Tarantapuff!" Ginger Jo said as she opened another sack of food.

When he wasn't eating, Sweetpuff loved to play outside with the other baby animals. One of his favorite games was hide-and-seek. He tried hiding in Smidge's pod, but that didn't work out well. Sweetpuff was kind of big.

Like all Tarantapuffs, Sweetpuff could spin webs. He liked to practice. Some of the Trolls in the village thought he was practicing too much—the sticky stuff got everywhere!

By the end of the day, Ginger Jo and Poppy were exhausted.

"I'm not sure I can do this again tomorrow," Poppy admitted.

"Me either," Ginger Jo said. "Sweetpuff is nice, but he sure needs a lot of attention!"

Luckily, someone who knew a lot about Tarantapuffs came by for a visit.

It was Bridget! To a Bergen like her, all Tarantapuffs were tiny and cute, even the full-grown ones.

"This little guy must have wandered off," she said. "He belongs with his family in the woods."

"But how will we find them?" Ginger Jo asked.

"We'll find 'em!" Bridget said confidently. "I know just the kinds of places Tarantapuffs like. Come on!"

Bridget led Ginger Jo, Poppy, and Sweetpuff through the woods. Soon they found two Tarantapuff parents. They were relieved to see Sweetpuff! The young Tarantapuff jumped off Bridget's finger and ran to his mom and dad.

"Aww, they look so happy!" Poppy said.

"I guess even Tarantapuffs love hugs!" Ginger Jo said.

"Definitely!" Poppy agreed.

"Bye, Sweetpuff!" Ginger Jo called as they left. "Come back and visit us! You're welcome any time!"

"No pet is really a problem," Poppy said to Bridget and Ginger Jo, "as long as you've got lots of love and patience . . . and plenty of room!"

By Rachel Chlebowski
Illustrated by Fabio Laguna and Alan Batson

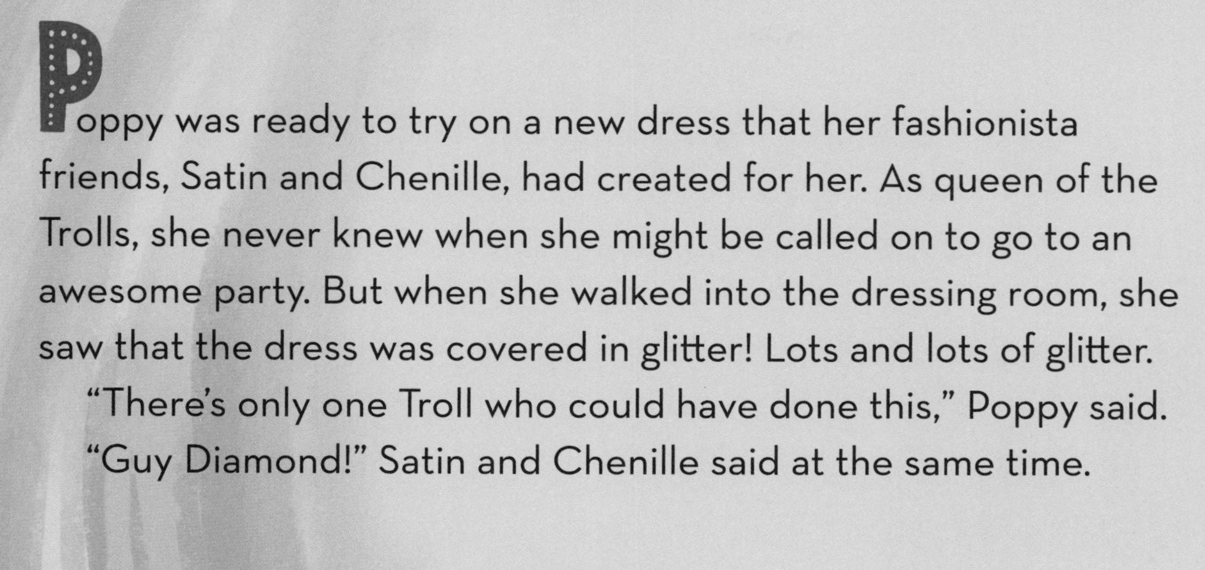

Poppy was ready to try on a new dress that her fashionista friends, Satin and Chenille, had created for her. As queen of the Trolls, she never knew when she might be called on to go to an awesome party. But when she walked into the dressing room, she saw that the dress was covered in glitter! Lots and lots of glitter.

"There's only one Troll who could have done this," Poppy said.

"Guy Diamond!" Satin and Chenille said at the same time.

“I’m going to find out what he’s up to!” Poppy said. “Luckily, Guy tends to leave a trail.”

She followed his glitter footprints into the garden—but no Guy Diamond.

Next, she searched the cupcakery. Biggie was making fancy treats. Glitter sparkled here and there—but no Guy Diamond.

Meanwhile, DJ Suki was mixing beats and making music with her Wooferbug.

"What is this tune missing?" she asked her Wooferbug.

"Glitter!" Guy Diamond sang, popping up out of nowhere. And with a poof, he covered everything in glitter.

"Yes! That's it!" she said. Her new tune sparkled with light.

But Guy Diamond left as quickly as he had appeared. DJ Suki was still jamming when Poppy arrived.

"I'm following the glitter to its source!" Poppy said.

"Well, he went thataway!" DJ Suki shouted over the music.

Then Poppy found Branch and Cooper.

"Guy glittered my harmonica," Cooper said. "Check this out!"

Cooper let loose on his harmonica. The brightest notes ever blew from it . . .

. . . and so did a lot of glitter, which landed right on Branch.

"I don't do glitter," Branch sighed, brushing off the sparkly dust.

"Well, come on, then," Poppy said, grabbing him by the arm. "Let's find out what all this glittering is about."

Poppy and Branch searched Troll Village high and low. Guy Diamond's trail of glitter was easy to follow, but Guy was hard to find!

Poppy and Branch almost caught up to Guy Diamond at Maddy's hair salon. Everyone there was covered in glitter.

"I guess Guy was just here," Poppy said.

"Yep," said one Troll.

"Sure was," said another.

"I saw him."

"How'd you guess?"

"I look amazing."

The Trolls decided to join Poppy's search party. At the edge of Troll Village, the glitter trail led deep into the dark forest. The group of Trolls stopped, but Poppy took a deep breath and bravely pushed the leaves aside.

"Oh my gah!" exclaimed Smidge.

It was a giant **GLITTER PARTY!**

"Welcome to the biggest, brightest, most glittering party ever!" Guy Diamond cheered as his friends joined in with their newly glittering clothing, hair, and accessories. "I'm so happy everyone could make it. And thank you for bringing the glitter!" he added with a wink.

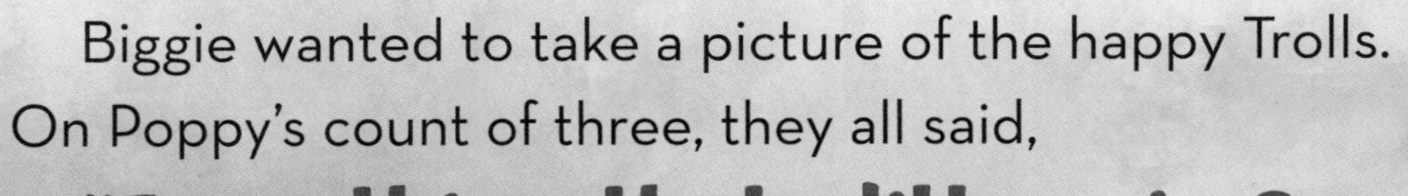

Biggie wanted to take a picture of the happy Trolls. On Poppy's count of three, they all said,

"Everything that glitters is Guy!"

Out of Branch's Bunker

By Mary Man-Kong
Illustrated by Character Building and Francesco Legramandi

This is Troll Village. It's where I live. Everybody is a little too happy here. They're all colorful, and they love to sing, and dance, and hug, and sing and dance, and hug and sing, and dance and hug. Everybody except . . .

I'm Branch, the only gray Troll. Unlike the other Trolls, I don't sing, I don't dance, and I don't hug. I mostly worry about the Bergens. They're big and mean and miserable. And a long time ago, they used to eat us.

See, the Bergens thought if they ate Trolls, they'd be as happy as Trolls. Luckily, clever King Peppy tricked the Bergens, and the Trolls were able to escape. Then they built a secret town, Troll Village, safely hidden from the Bergens.

But the Bergens might come back at any time, so I keep my guard up. I stomp at everyone's noisy parties, telling them, "BE QUIET! You will attract the Bergens!" And then I go back to my safe and well-hidden bunker.

Today there's a celebration. The whole town is throwing the biggest, craziest, loudest party ever!

And no matter how much WARNING I do, nobody listens.

Princess Poppy believes everything is cupcakes and rainbows.

She loves to sing . . . and dance . . . and sing. And the louder, the better.

They all just keep singing and dancing, and hugging and singing, and dancing and hugging, and they have glitter and rainbows and DJ music and **FIREWORKS** and . . .

. . . a **BERGEN**! The Bergen Chef hears us and comes stomping through our town. She snatches up a bunch of our friends and takes them back to Bergen Town.

But I have prepared for this day. I created the best hiding place in the universe: a super-secret survival bunker. It has enough food and water to last me ten years—eleven if I'm willing to store and drink my own sweat, *which I am*.

I'm all set until Poppy shows up. She's trying to come up with a plan to rescue her friends, and asks for my help. Then she borrows my entire bunker for the rest of the Trolls to hide in! *ARGHHHH!*

All those happy Trolls make me CRAZY! So I go with Poppy to save her friends. We travel through the dark forest and have to battle weird monsters and scary spiders. But Poppy has a unique way of getting things done—nothing can slow her down. By working together, we soon find the secret tunnels to the Troll Tree in Bergen Town.

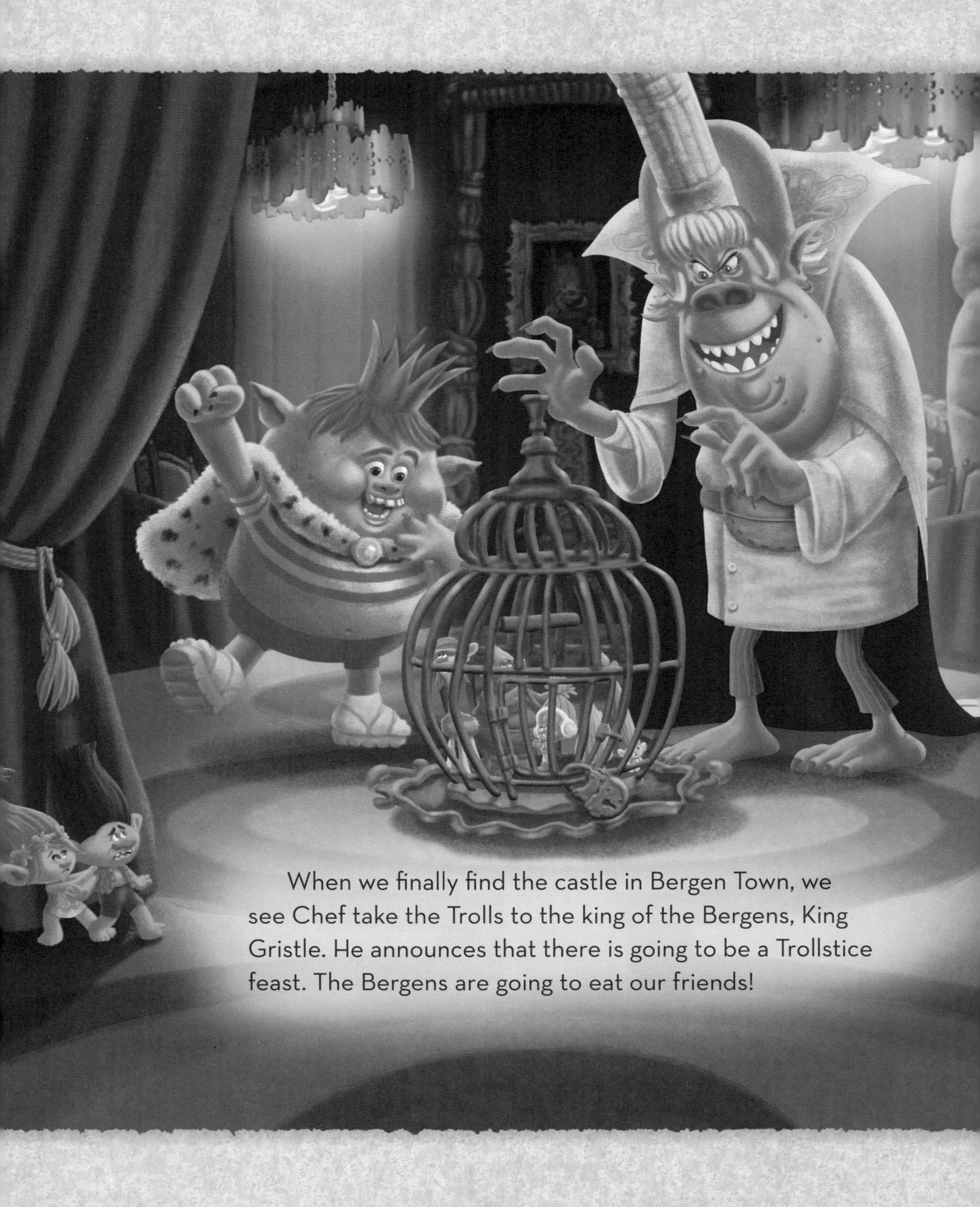

When we finally find the castle in Bergen Town, we see Chef take the Trolls to the king of the Bergens, King Gristle. He announces that there is going to be a Trollstice feast. The Bergens are going to eat our friends!

A Bergen maid named Bridget is keeping the Trolls in her room. Poppy comes up with a smart idea. She sees that Bridget has a mad, crazy crush on King Gristle. If the Trolls can help Bridget find the confidence to win over King Gristle, then she can help us escape Bergen Town!

When Bridget meets King Gristle, she introduces herself as Lady Glittersparkles. With a little coaching from Poppy, Bridget tells King Gristle how she feels about him. That's when he shows her his locket—with Creek inside!

Poppy would never leave any Troll behind, so we sneak into King Gristle's room to rescue our friend. We grab the locket and zoom out of there.

But when we open the locket, Creek isn't there! Sadly, we learn that Creek told Chef where the other Trolls are, in order to save his own life. Now we're all doomed! **DOOMED!**

I've never seen Poppy so miserable. She doesn't dance, hug, or sing. She doesn't even want to scrapbook!

Poppy becomes totally gray, just like me. Soon all the Trolls turn gray as they lose hope one by one.

That's when I realize Poppy is my best friend. She makes me crazy with all her singing and hugging and dancing and cupcakes and rainbows, but she also makes me happy. It's hard to see her so sad.

I can't believe what I'm about to do. I take a deep breath and—oh, boy—I start to sing. Before I know it, Poppy gets her color back! All the other Trolls get their color back, too—and so do I!

Then Bridget finds us! She decides she can't let us get eaten, so she helps us escape.

We can't abandon Bridget, so we save her—Troll-style! When King Gristle learns that Bridget is really Lady Glittersparkles, he realizes that he's in love with her, which makes him truly happy. He doesn't need to eat Trolls after all!

We start singing and dancing. The Bergens are confused at first, but then they join in. Just like me, they discover that their happiness has been trapped inside them all along.

Everyone—Trolls and Bergens alike—cheers! After that, Poppy becomes queen of the Trolls, and we have the biggest, loudest, craziest party ever!

And you know what? **I LOVE IT!**

The Sound of Spring

By David Lewman

Illustrated by Fabio Laguna and Alan Batson

It was a warm spring night in Troll Village. All the Trolls were sleeping—except Branch. He was wide awake. He kept hearing something.

“What is that sound?” Branch said to himself.

He looked everywhere in his bunker. He looked in boxes. He looked on shelves. He looked in the hamper.

But he couldn’t find anything!

After a long sleepless night, Branch went to Troll Village. All the Trolls were going about their business.

Branch still heard the sound.

He checked around the village, but he couldn't figure out where the sound was coming from.

The sound was driving him **crazy**!

Then Branch saw Cloud Guy. He asked if Cloud Guy heard the sound, too.

Cloud Guy stopped and listened.

Cloud Guy heard it!
"Hey," he said, "maybe *you're* making the sound."
"No way!" said Branch.
"Yeah, it's you," said Cloud Guy. "You're chirping!"

Branch thought Cloud Guy was playing a trick on him.

"I am not chirping!" he exclaimed. He was so angry that he chased Cloud Guy through the woods to make him take back his words.

"Chirp!
Chirp!
Chirp!" Cloud Guy called.

Branch chased Cloud Guy all the way to Poppy's house.

Poppy was busy in her garden when she heard all the noise.

"What's going on?" she asked.

"I keep hearing a chirping sound," explained Branch. "And it's driving me crazy!"

Poppy listened. She didn't hear anything . . . at first. Then she got closer to Branch and listened hard.

Chirp! Chirp! Chirp!

She knew where the sound was coming from!

Poppy reached into Branch's hair—and pulled out an egg!

"This is where the chirping is coming from," said Poppy. "A bird must have laid an egg in your hair!"

Branch couldn't believe it!

"And I think the egg is about to hatch!" exclaimed Poppy. She quickly put the egg back into Branch's hair.

Suddenly, a baby bird popped out of the egg. Then it began to sing. Poppy and Branch began to sing, too.

The little bird's mother heard her baby singing, and soon came flying back. They all sang a happy tune together. When they were finished, the mother and her baby bird flew off.

The Trolls waved goodbye to the birds.

"Aww, that baby bird was so cute," said Poppy. "And it made such pretty chirping sounds."

"Yeah," agreed Branch. "I'm going to miss the chirping a little bit—but not *too* much!"

By Mary Man-Kong

I'm **Branch**! We Trolls love big parties and having fun. We even like spooky stuff, so every year on Troll-o-ween, we dress up and have a big, loud celebration.

We used to think the Bergens were the scariest things in the world, but now we're friends with them. There are plenty of other things to be scared of, though—just look at my scrapbook!

Lots of spooky things live in the dark forest around Troll Village—for instance, the big Tarantapuffs that tried to eat Poppy! Those weird eyes and long legs get me every time! Totally spooky!

Then there's the three-eyed creature that also tried to eat Poppy! And the really big green guy that wanted to snap her up! The list of scary—and hungry—creatures goes on. . . .

One time, Biggie got scared by some other weird creatures.
One swallowed another.
Then some birds ate that thing.
Then THAT thing caught on fire—and got eaten by something else!

But spooky things don't always eat things or catch on fire. Sometimes they're just hanging out.

I may have found my true colors, but I still don't trust these guys!

Back when we Trolls thought the Bergens were spooky, I admit it: I was pretty terrified of them, too. But we learned that the Bergens weren't scary at all. They just needed to find the happiness inside themselves.

But, for me, the scariest thing is still . . .
HUG TIME!
Aaahhhh!

Happy Troll-o-ween!